"I DON'T LIKE CHOOSE YOUR OWN ADVENTURE® BOOKS. I *LOVE* THEM!" says Jessica Gordon, age ten. And now, kids between the ages of six and nine can choose their own adventures too. Here's what kids have to say about the Skylark Choose Your Own Adventure® books.

"These are my favorite books because you can pick whatever choice you want—and the story is all about you."
—**Katy Alson,** *age 8*

"I love finding out how my story will end."
—**Joss Williams,** *age 9*

"I like all the illustrations!"
—**Savitri Brightfield,** *age 7*

"A six-year-old friend and I have lots of fun making the decisions together."
—**Peggy Marcus** *(adult)*

Bantam Skylark Books in the Choose Your Own
    Adventure® Series
Ask your bookseller for the books you have missed

THE MUMMY'S TOMB

STEPHANIE SPINNER

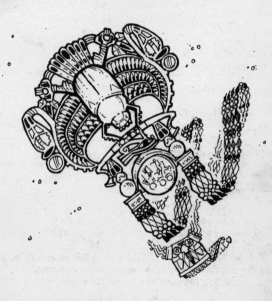

ILLUSTRATED BY TED ENIK

An Edward Packard Book

A BANTAM SKYLARK BOOK®
TORONTO · NEW YORK · LONDON · SYDNEY · AUCKLAND

RL 2, 007–009

THE MUMMY'S TOMB
A Bantam Skylark Book / February 1985

Original conception of Edward Packard

ISBN 0-553-15294-7

PRINTED IN THE UNITED STATES OF AMERICA

CW   0 9 8 7 6 5 4 3 2 1

To Karina

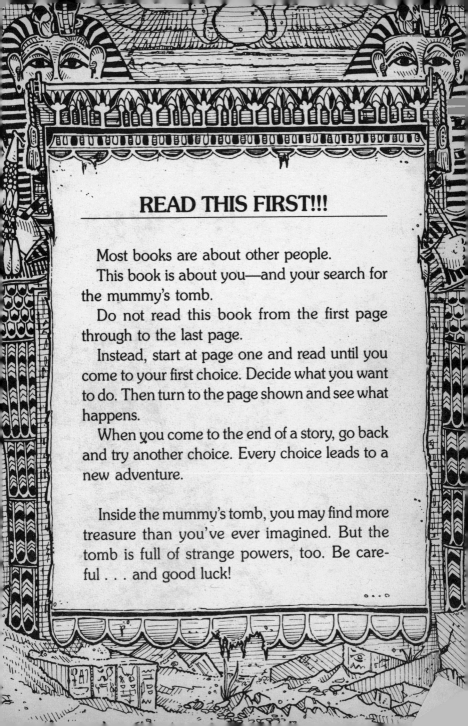

READ THIS FIRST!!!

Most books are about other people.

This book is about you—and your search for the mummy's tomb.

Do not read this book from the first page through to the last page.

Instead, start at page one and read until you come to your first choice. Decide what you want to do. Then turn to the page shown and see what happens.

When you come to the end of a story, go back and try another choice. Every choice leads to a new adventure.

Inside the mummy's tomb, you may find more treasure than you've ever imagined. But the tomb is full of strange powers, too. Be careful . . . and good luck!

"Fasten your seat belts, please," says a voice **1** over the loudspeaker. "Flight 216 to Cairo is now ready for takeoff."

The jet soars into the clouds, and you think again how lucky you are. You're on your way to Egypt with your aunt Dottie. She's an archaeologist—someone who studies ancient civilizations. Mummies are her specialty.

Dottie is searching for a necklace that was buried thousands of years ago in the tomb of a Pharaoh—an ancient Egyptian king. She's described it to you many times. It's golden, and in its center is a crystal scarab—a special charm worn by the ancient Egyptians.

Now, as you fly toward Egypt, she tells you why she wants to find the necklace so much.

Turn to page 2.

2   "The scarab has powers," she explains. "Amazing, magical ones. People say it can grant wishes and reveal the future. Even send its owner through time!"

Just then you notice a man staring at you from across the aisle. When your eyes meet, he turns away quickly. Is it your imagination, or is that a gun under his jacket?

Very quietly, you point him out to your aunt. She looks worried. "He's a member of Al-Fazi's gang," she says. "They're smugglers. They want to find the necklace, too."

After the plane lands, you and your aunt wait at the baggage counter for your luggage. You see the man from the plane standing at the edge of a crowd of passengers. This time you know you're not imagining things. He's following you!

If you try to lose Al-Fazi's man by heading straight for the desert, turn to page 5.

If you head for the hotel first, turn to page 6.

You and your aunt hurry out of the airport. A **5** taxi takes you to your aunt's jeep, and soon you're speeding toward the desert. You drive all day. At dusk you pass a tiny village. Then you come to a high pyramid that stands in front of a rocky cliff.

Your aunt pulls a wrinkled map out of her pocket. "If this map is right," she says, "the tomb we're looking for isn't under the pyramid. It's inside that cliff." She points to an entrance that's cut right into the rock wall.

A bright moon rises. Since it's so late, you and Dottie decide to set up camp and get some sleep. You can start exploring early in the morning.

You climb into your sleeping bags. Moments later, Dottie is snoring gently. But you just can't fall asleep. Finally you decide to take a look at the tomb site on your own. You pick up your flashlight and set off toward the cliff.

Turn to page 9.

6   You and your aunt leave the airport as fast as you can. On the street, you hail a taxi and climb in. Dottie looks out the rear window nervously as you make your way slowly through the crowded streets of Cairo.

"It looks as if we've lost him," you say.

"I'm not so sure," she replies, as the taxi pulls up at the hotel. "There's a good chance that Al-Fazi's men are watching us. They might try to follow us to the tomb tomorrow. I think we'd better change our plans—fast!"

Turn to page 16.

It doesn't take you long to find the opening in the cliff wall. You crawl inside and shine your flashlight around. You're in a dark, narrow passageway that leads steeply down. You walk along until you come to a tunnel so low that your head brushes the ceiling. Finally the floor becomes level, and you turn a corner.

On your right you see a door with a scarab painted on it. Suddenly a strange curtain of flames blazes up in front of the door. Your aunt has told you that magic forces protect the mummy's tomb. These flames are bright—but they don't give off any heat! You wonder if you should try to pass through them.

On your left you see another doorway. On it is a painting of a Pharaoh, and he's wearing a scarab necklace! Something tells you this is the entrance to the mummy's tomb. But wait—is that a scorpion on the wall over the doorway?

If you try to walk through the flames, turn to page 12.

If you try the other door, turn to page 14.

10 The necklace gleams in the darkness. The scarab looks as if it's glowing. Suddenly you want more than anything to put the necklace on.

When you reach for it, the scarab flashes and then grows dim. If the necklace is magical, maybe you'd better not put it on. You could just bring it back to your aunt and show it to her. Or you could leave it on the mummy and come back for it some other time.

If you decide to put the necklace on, turn to page 27.

If you decide to bring the necklace back to your aunt, turn to page 21.

If you decide to leave the necklace on the mummy, turn to page 39.

Finally you tumble to a stop. You're not hurt, **11** only winded. But when you find Dottie, she's lying still. Her leg is bent at a strange angle.

You think of a village you passed while you were driving. Maybe you should try to find your way out of the cliff. Then you could look for help in the village. But it might be safer to stay where you are until morning.

If you try to find a way out, turn to page 30.

If you stay with your aunt until daybreak,
turn to page 24.

12   You dash through the flames. They don't burn at all! When you reach the door, you push it as hard as you can. The door opens slowly, and you step inside.

You turn on your flashlight. The first thing you see is a giant gold mummy case resting on a platform. On either side of it are two fierce-looking golden lions. Below the lions are many statues made of gold and glittering with gems.

You step closer to the platform. You've got to know if the mummy inside the case is wearing the magic necklace!

Turn to page 20.

14 You start to pull at the door. It's locked! Then something drops onto your arm. You jump back, but it's too late. You feel a sharp sting. An icy coldness creeps through your body, and you drop to the ground.

Turn to page 54.

You try to go back to your aunt. But you must **15** have taken a wrong turn.

Which way should you go? You light a match and look around. The first thing you see is a scarab painted on the wall next to you.

Could you be near the mummy's burial chamber? You decide to find out.

Turn to page 42.

16   You and your aunt decide to set out for the tomb right away. Late that night you sneak out of the hotel and take off in her jeep. You drive for hours through the silent desert. Just as you reach the tomb site, a blinding sandstorm comes up. You can hardly see. Suddenly a huge, dark shape looms up in front of you.

"I think that's the cliff we're looking for—the one with the tomb inside it," shouts Dottie over the howling wind. "Let's run for it!" You dash for the cliff and grope around for an entrance.

Your aunt stumbles and falls.

"Aunt Dottie?" you call. She doesn't answer. Then you hear a scream—and a thud! Suddenly you're sliding down a dark shaft.

Turn to page 11.

18   You turn and run faster than you ever have in your life! You go up the stairs and down a long corridor. You pass a hall lined with frowning animal-headed statues.

Finally you duck into a doorway.

You're in a room piled high with treasure.

There are giant mummy cases, golden statues, and precious jewels all around you.

It looks as if you've found the Pharaoh's burial chamber. Now all you've got to do is find your aunt!

The End

20   But when you touch the lid of the case you hear a low, eerie voice. "Beware!" it sighs. "Who opens the case of the mummy will be cursed for all time."

What should you do? You'd really like to know if you've found the magic necklace. But the mummy's curse may be a very powerful one.

If you ignore the warning and open the mummy case, turn to page 47.

If you listen to the warning and take other treasure out of the tomb instead, turn to page 51.

You put the necklace in your pocket and use your rope to climb back up the shaft. You're walking along the tunnel when you stumble on a loose rock and drop your flashlight. It goes out.

You grope around in the darkness, but you can't find it. Suddenly the ground crumbles under your feet. You fall, slide, and land with a splash in a pool of water.

Choking and sputtering, you sit up and look around. Then you see them—crocodiles!

Turn to page 48.

You use your climbing rope to lower yourself down the shaft. When you reach the ground, all you find is a wall of rocks and rubble. Have you come to a dead end?

Maybe not. When you look at the wall more closely, you spot a small opening. You dig at it with your hands until it's big enough for you to squeeze through.

Go on to the next page.

You turn on your flashlight and look around. **23** You can't believe your eyes. You're surrounded by treasure! There are bowls, goblets, statues, and even chairs made of gold. And in the center of the room is a golden mummy case!

Inside the case is a mummy wearing a golden mask. And around its neck is a collar made of golden beads, with a crystal scarab in the center.

You've found the magic necklace!

Turn to page 10.

24   You sit down near your aunt and wait for daylight. Suddenly you see a light flickering above your head. As you watch, a rope comes down the shaft. Then a man slides down the rope and lands only a few feet away from you.

You hold your breath when you recognize him. He's the man who was following you in the airport this morning!

The man pulls out a piece of paper. You can't see it very well, but it looks like a map. He heads off down a narrow tunnel.

You're sitting there, wondering what to do, when you hear a terrible scream!

Turn to page 28.

You just can't resist. You pull the necklace off the mummy and put it on. It feels very heavy. And in a moment, so do you. Soon your body starts to tingle, and you grow weak. Then your eyes close. You fall to the floor.

When you wake up, you hear distant voices. But something's wrong—you can't see, and you can't move. You're wrapped in bands of cloth from head to foot!

"Look at this case, Junior," says a woman's voice. "Just imagine. There's a real mummy inside it! It's probably thousands of years old!"

"Mom, I'm tired of this museum," answers another voice. "Let's go now. I want some ice cream."

The voices drift away as you lie there.

The magic necklace turned you into a mummy!

The End

28   You run down the narrow tunnel and hear another scream. Then you stop—just in time.

You're on the edge of a deep pit. At the bottom, standing on a fallen statue, is the man. Hundreds of writhing snakes are crawling toward him.

The man's eyes are filled with terror. When he sees you, he screams again. You don't understand the words he uses, but you know he's asking you to help.

You could throw him one end of your climbing rope. But he has a long, gleaming knife. And there's a good chance he might use it against you!

If you help the man, turn to page 36.

If you run back to your aunt, turn to page 15.

30   You decide to look for a way out. You take your climbing rope and your flashlight and set off down a steep path. At the end of the path you see two doorways carved into the stone walls.

At first they look exactly the same. But when you step closer, you see that one doorway has a painting of a jackal over it. The other has a painting of a cobra over it.

Which should you choose?

If you choose the doorway with the jackal over it, turn to page 40.

If you choose the doorway with the cobra over it, turn to page 34.

You jump over the crocodile and land in front **33**
of the small opening. The crocodiles snap at you
hungrily, but they can't reach you.

With a sigh of relief, you lean back against the
wall. Suddenly it starts moving! You must have
leaned against a secret door!

When the wall finally stops moving, you're
alone in the dark. But in the distance you see a
tiny speck of light. You crawl toward the light. It
gets brighter and brighter until you find an
opening in the tunnel wall that you can squeeze
through. You're outside!

The first thing you see is Dottie's jeep surrounded by a crowd of curious villagers. They
help you rescue your aunt.

"It looks as if we won't be able to look for the
Pharaoh's necklace for a while," says Dottie
sadly. Her leg is broken. She'll be wearing a cast
for weeks.

You smile. "Have I got a surprise for you!"
you say.

The End

34   Just beyond the doorway with the cobra on it is a long, low tunnel. At the end of the tunnel you find a square opening cut into the dirt floor. It looks like a shaft that leads underground.

Your aunt has told you that Pharaohs were often buried in small chambers hidden deep beneath the ground. You've got your climbing rope and your flashlight. If you go down the shaft, you might find the mummy's tomb!

But you can't see where the shaft ends, or what's at the bottom of it. Maybe you'd better not go down alone.

If you climb down the shaft, turn to page 22.

If you decide to go back out the door and try again, turn to page 40.

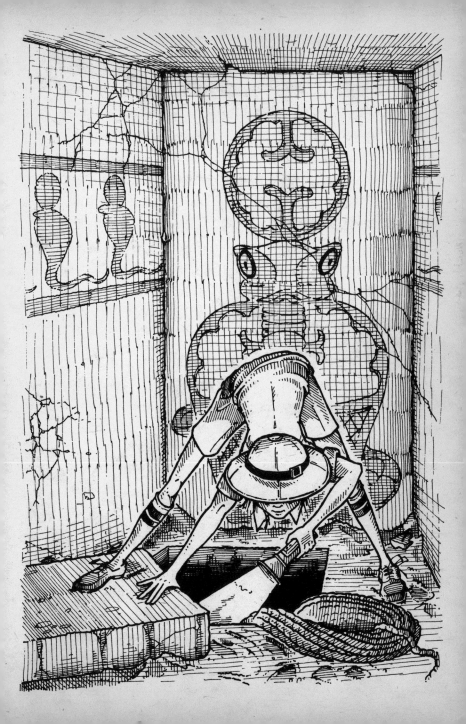

36   You throw the man your rope. He pulls himself up out of the pit. Then he hands you the map and faints dead away.

You follow the map until you come to a low stone doorway. When you walk inside, the first thing you see is a giant golden mummy case. And it's open. This must be the Pharaoh's tomb!

You look inside the case. There, as if it's been waiting for you, is the Pharaoh's mummy—wearing the scarab necklace!

You lift off the necklace and carry it back to your aunt. She's awake now, and very glad to see you.

She reads the ancient writing carved on it: "Use force to find the necklace, and it will curse you. Use good will to find it, and its blessings will be yours forever."

The End

Slowly you draw away from the necklace. "It **39** belongs here," you think. "On the mummy."

You're about to leave the burial chamber when you notice a beautiful golden chair near the entrance. You pick up the golden scepter that's lying across the seat. Then you sit down in the chair. "I wonder if this was the Pharaoh's throne," you think as you settle back.

A wonderful drowsy feeling comes over you. Your eyes close and you fall asleep.

When you wake up, you feel as if you've slept for years. You stretch lazily and look around.

You're lying on a huge canopied bed. Dark-haired, smiling servants are gathered around you. One of them asks you what you'd like to eat and drink.

You sit up, speechless. You're in ancient Egypt! And from the way everyone is acting, you must be very important.

You find out just how important you are when a servant bows deeply and places a crown on your head. You have become the Pharaoh!

The End

40   Inside the door with the jackal on it, there is a steep stone stairway. The stairs twist and wind downward, and the lower you climb, the darker it gets.

You hear faint sounds. Are they whispers? Sighs? You're not sure. You wonder where you're going.

Then you hear an even stranger noise. It sounds like—it is!—the clatter of bones!

If you decide to keep going, turn to page 44.

If you decide to turn back, turn to page 24.

42 There is an opening in the wall underneath the sign of the scarab. By digging with your hands, you make the opening larger. Soon you can crawl through to the other side.

The first thing you see is a golden mummy case on a platform. But just as you reach for the lid you hear a low rumbling sound. It gets louder and louder.

Dust and rocks start to fall. Something—you're not sure what—has started a rockslide. Now the wall of the chamber is caving in. You're trapped!

Then you hear another sound—a strange, low creaking. You turn around quickly. As you watch, the cover of the mummy case slowly starts to rise. The next thing you see is an arm wrapped in ragged bandages.

It's the mummy. And it's reaching out—for you!

The End

When the stairway ends, you find yourself in a huge stone chamber. It's damp and gloomy. At the far end you see a throne with someone sitting on it. It's a man with a jackal's head!

"Why have you come to the Kingdom of the Dead?" he snarls. You look around and see that the chamber is filled with skeletons.

Turn to page 18.

You pull open the lid of the mummy case. **47**
There, wrapped in musty cloth, is the mummy.
Around its neck is a beautiful golden collar with
a crystal scarab in the center. You've found the
magic necklace!

Suddenly the lid of the mummy case comes
crashing down. It closes with a loud THUD—as
if someone, or something, had pushed it!

Then you hear a soft whisper. "Now suffer
the curse of the mummy!" something hisses.

All at once you feel weak. Your head reels.
You fall to the floor.

When you open your eyes, you're outside
under a blazing sun. You hear the angry crack-
ing of a whip and groans from everyone around
you.

You look up. Towering above you is a huge
unfinished pyramid.

Now you understand the mummy's curse.
You've been sent back to ancient Egypt as a
slave. You will spend the rest of your days build-
ing a pyramid!

The End

48   The crocodiles glide toward you, their eyes gleaming. You've got to get away *fast*.

On one side of the pool you see a small opening in the rock wall. You could run for it. But you'd have to jump over a crocodile's back to get to it.

On the other side of the pool you see a stone post. If you worked quickly, you could lasso the post with your rope and pull yourself out of the pool.

If you jump over a crocodile to get to the opening in the wall, turn to page 33.

If you use your climbing rope as a lasso, turn to page 52.

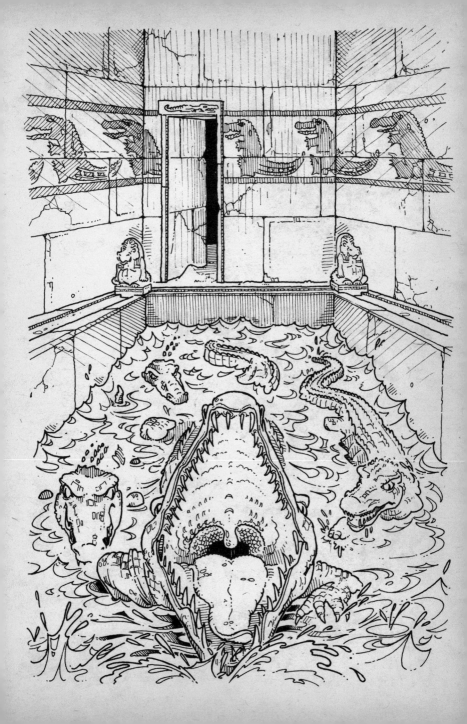

You decide you'd better not risk the mummy's curse. Instead you choose a small golden statue of a cat to show to your aunt. Then you leave the chamber and climb back up to the opening in the cliff. Before long you're shaking Dottie awake.

You show her the cat. Her eyes fly open. Then she grins and jumps out of her sleeping bag. "That cat is all the proof I need," she says. "We've come to the right place." She gathers her tools together and runs off toward the cliff.

"Come on!" she shouts over her shoulder. "Let's get back to the tomb right away. We can sleep some other time!"

The End

52   The crocodiles slither toward you, but your aim is good. You lasso the post and pull yourself out of the pool just in time.

Ahead of you are many dark, winding passageways. Which one will lead you back to your aunt? You wish you knew.

Then you remember the necklace. Maybe its magic will help you. You hold it in both hands, close your eyes, and think, "Take me back to my aunt."

It works! When your eyes open, you're with Aunt Dottie again.

You shake her gently until she wakes up. Then she winces. "My leg!" she gasps. "I must have hurt it when I fell. Are you all right?"

"I'm fine," you tell her. Just as you start to show her the necklace, you hear voices. A group of villagers appears far above you at the top of the shaft. Before long they've helped you and your aunt to safety.

You alone know the power of the scarab necklace.

Will you tell the world?

Or will it be your secret forever?

The End

54   When you wake up, you see your aunt bending over you. She has a worried frown on her face. You realize you're in a hospital bed!

"It's a good thing I found you when I did," she says. "Scorpion bites can be fatal!"

"But what about the tomb? And the necklace?" you ask.

"Too dangerous—at least for you," says Aunt Dottie. "I'm shipping you back home just as soon as you can walk!"

The End

ABOUT THE AUTHOR

Stephanie Spinner grew up in New York City and attended college in Vermont. She is a children's book editor who has also written several children's books, as well as many articles on Tibetan painting. Ms. Spinner has traveled all over the world and has spent many happy hours in the Cairo airport. She now lives in New York City.

ABOUT THE ILLUSTRATOR

Ted Enik is a playwright, set designer, magazine artist, and cartoonist as well as a children's book illustrator. He is the illustrator of the Sherluck Bones Mystery-Detective books, which were written by Jim and Mary Razzi and published by Bantam Books. He has also illustrated *The Curse of Batterslea Hall* in Bantam's Choose Your Own Adventure series. In the Bantam Skylark Choose Your Own Adventure series, he has illustrated *The Creature From Miller's Pond* and *Summer Camp*. Mr. Enik lives in New York City.